# Dear Parents:

Congratulations! Your child is taking the first steps on an exciting journey. The destination? Independent reading!

**STEP INTO READING®** will help your child get there. The program offers five steps to reading success. Each step includes fun stories and colorful art or photographs. In addition to original fiction and books with favorite characters, there are Step into Reading Non-Fiction Readers, Phonics Readers and Boxed Sets, Sticker Readers, and Comic Readers—a complete literacy program with something to interest every child.

## Learning to Read, Step by Step!

**Ready to Read  Preschool–Kindergarten**
**• big type and easy words • rhyme and rhythm • picture clues**
For children who know the alphabet and are eager to begin reading.

**Reading with Help  Preschool–Grade 1**
**• basic vocabulary • short sentences • simple stories**
For children who recognize familiar words and sound out new words with help.

**Reading on Your Own  Grades 1–3**
**• engaging characters • easy-to-follow plots • popular topics**
For children who are ready to read on their own

**Reading Paragraphs  Grades 2–3**
**• challenging vocabulary • short paragraphs • exciting stories**
For newly independent readers who read simple sentences with confidence.

**Ready for Chapters  Grades 2–4**
**• chapters • longer paragraphs • full-color art**
For children who want to take the plunge into chapter books but still like colorful pictures.

**STEP INTO READING®** is designed to give every child a successful reading experience. The grade levels are only guides; children will progress through the steps at their own speed, developing confidence in their reading.

Remember, a lifetime love of reading starts with a single step!

Thomas the Tank Engine & Friends™

CREATED BY BRITT ALLCROFT

Based on The Railway Series by The Reverend W Awdry.
 Published in the United States by Random House Children's Books, a division of Random House LLC, 1745 Broadway, New York, NY 10019, and in Canada by Random House of Canada Limited, Toronto, Penguin Random House Companies.



Visit us on the Web!
StepIntoReading.com
randomhouse.com/kids
www.thomasandfriends.com

Educators and librarians, for a variety of teaching tools, visit us at RHTeachersLibrarians.com

ISBN 978-0-385-37387-6 (trade) — ISBN 978-0-375-97210-2 (lib. bdg.) —
ISBN 978-0-375-98212-5 (ebook)

Printed in the United States of America
10 9 8 7 6 5 4 3

Random House Children's Books supports the First Amendment
and celebrates the right to read.

STEP 1 READY TO READ

STEP INTO READING®

THOMAS & FRIENDS™

# SANTA'S LITTLE ENGINE

Based on The Railway Series
by The Reverend W Awdry

Illustrated by Tom LaPadula

Random House New York

Christmas on the
Island of Sodor!
Plow, Thomas, plow!

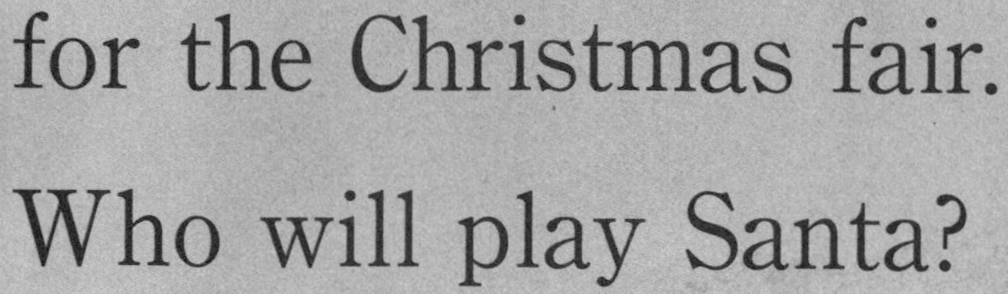

It is time
for the Christmas fair.
Who will play Santa?

Sir Topham Hatt!

Santa needs a sled.

Workers hammer.

Painters paint.

Winston does not
look like a sled.

Thomas picks up
a real sled.

CRANKY

Uh-oh! Ice!

Thomas goes slow.

*Peep, peep!*

The sled is safe.

# Where is Santa?

Ho, ho, ho!

Santa is ready.
Thomas backs up.

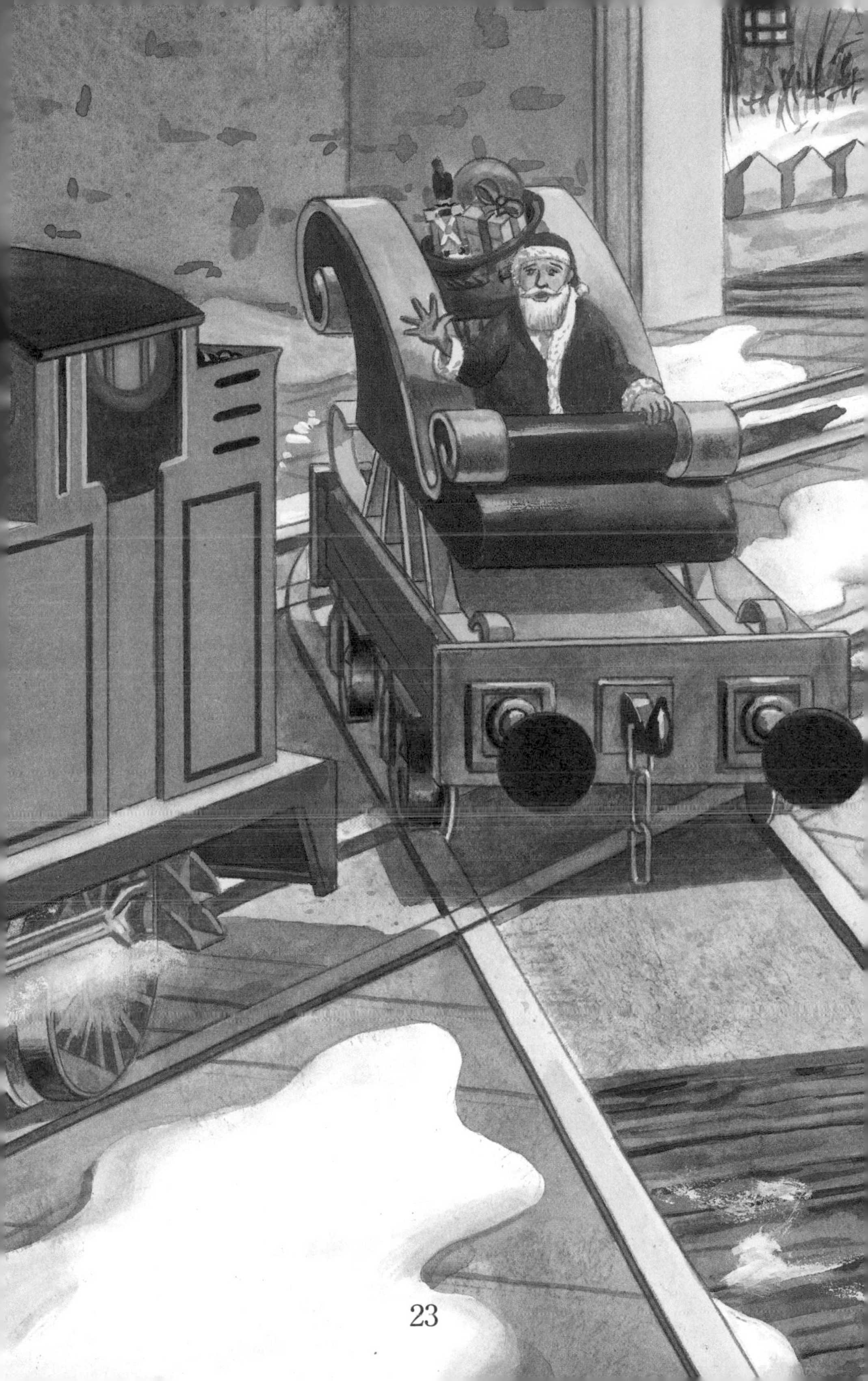

Watch out,

Thomas!

Oh, no!

He bumps the sled!

Thomas will save Santa.

Hurry, Thomas!

Look out
for branches!

*Peep, peep!*

Ho, ho, ho!

Thomas pulls
Santa's sled.

Merry Christmas!